Wayne

Something In The Water — Book Three

Lorri Ryan Oliver

Tribury Media LLC
Middlebury, Connecticut

Published by Tribury Media LLC, Middlebury, Connecticut
This is a work of fiction. Names, characters, places and incidents are products of the author's imagination or are used fictitiously.

This is a work of original fiction. The author used standard digital tools, including AI, for research, continuity, story development, and editing.

Lorri Ryan Oliver is a pen name.

ISBN: 979-8-9953431-4-1
First Edition, 2026
Also available as an ebook wherever ebooks are sold.

This story begins here.

Read slowly. Step over nothing.

Wayne

Something In The Water — Book Three

The Phone Call

He called on a Thursday.

I was in the office at Amorous, going over the week's numbers with the particular attention I give them on Thursdays, which is to say half my attention, the other half distributed among the music Ginny had put on in the other room — something unhurried from the cubbies, Chet Baker if I was placing it correctly, which I probably was — and the memory of a May evening two weeks prior that had not stopped replaying at inconvenient moments.

The phone showed *Wayne X.* I looked at it for one ring. Then I picked up.

"Good timing," I said.

"Is it?"

"Chet Baker and a slow Thursday. Yes."

A pause — the comfortable kind, the kind that doesn't need filling. Wayne had a craftsman's ease with silence. He didn't apologize for it and he didn't rush it.

"I've been thinking about coming back up," he said. "If there's a weekend that works."

"There are several weekends that work," I said.

"Any particular one."

"The one where you come," I said. "That one works."

He laughed — low and warm, the laugh that meant he was pleased and wasn't going to make a production of being pleased. "Curtis House again, probably."

"Skip Curtis House," I said. "Try the Butterfly Inn. It's on Main Street, two minutes from Amorous."

"Butterfly Inn."

"Victorian. Wraparound porch. Gourmet breakfast included." I considered. "It's straight out of Gilmore Girls — the woman even has a daughter in college."

A pause. "I don't know what that is."

"I know you don't," I said. "The only thing missing is Luke's Coffee Shop."

"I could be Luke," he said.

He had no idea what he'd just said. Which was exactly right.

"Come on a Friday," I said. "Stay through Sunday. Bring the Impala — the weather should hold."

"I'll call them today."

"Do that." I leaned back in the office chair. "And Wayne."

"Yes."

"I think," I said, "that you only want to come back so you can feel me up."

The pause this time was different. A beat. The craftsman considering the material.

"There's that," he said.

"The kissing booth," I said, "doesn't have an upper limit. Just so you know."

The silence that followed was the longest of the call. Not empty — full. A man sitting with something and finding it worth sitting with.

"Good to know," he said finally. Quietly.

"It is good to know," I agreed. "I'll put on Chet Baker when you arrive. *She Was Too Good To Me.* 1974. Do you know it?"

"I'll know it when I hear it," he said.

"Yes," I said. "You will."

* * *

I set the phone down and looked at the office for a moment — the desk, the numbers I hadn't finished, the doorway to the kitchen where Martin was doing something that smelled like a brown butter situation — and thought about June.

There would be a Wayne weekend in June.

I went back to the numbers. In the other room, Chet Baker played on. Through the doorway I could hear Ginny setting up the bar with the efficient choreography of a woman whose hands know the work without consulting her. Glass, glass, glass. The soft percussion of a Thursday evening beginning.

I would need to think about the blouse.

The Bistro Table

I called Cynthia on Saturday morning.

Not texted — called. Cynthia knows the difference. A text from me means information. A call means something is happening and I've decided she should know about it.

She picked up on the second ring.

"Lorri."

"Are you busy."

"I'm doing laundry," she said. "Which means I'm not busy."

"Come for coffee," I said. "Eleven."

A pause — shorter than Wayne's, different in character. Cynthia's pauses are computational. She was already filing things, cross-referencing, arriving at a preliminary conclusion. "I'll be there at ten-fifty," she said.

She was there at ten-fifty.

* * *

Cynthia Mary Ryan is two years younger than me and has known me for all of those two years plus fifty-nine of mine, which means she has known me longer than anyone alive and reads me with the particular fluency of someone who learned the language in childhood and has never stopped practicing. She came through the door in jeans and a sweater with her dark hair pulled back and her reading glasses on top of her head and the expression of a woman who already knows she's about to get information and is pretending she stopped by for coffee.

I had the coffee ready. We sat at the bistro table in my kitchen — the small one, the one that means face to face with nowhere to look that isn't each other — and she wrapped both hands around her mug and looked at me.

"Well," she said.

"Well what," I said.

"You called me on a Saturday morning and told me to come for coffee," she said. "So. Well."

I looked at my coffee. I looked at Cynthia. I thought about how long she'd been filing things — the car show story last October, the drive-in in May, whatever I had and hadn't said across the months in between. She'd been patient. Cynthia is precise even when she's being patient, which means her patience has a deadline.

"Wayne Xavier is coming next weekend," I said.

She nodded once, slowly. Filing confirmed.

"He called Thursday," I said. "He's staying at the Butterfly Inn. Friday through Sunday."

"The Butterfly Inn," she said.

"On Main Street. Two minutes from Amorous."

"I know where the Butterfly Inn is," she said. Not sharp — observational. She let a moment pass. "How long has this been going on."

"Going on," I said, "implies a progression I haven't fully mapped."

"Lorri."

"The drive-in was May," I said. "The booth was the night after."

Her expression didn't change, exactly. Something behind it did. She was recalibrating — not surprised, recalibrating. There's a difference. "The booth," she said.

"My booth. At Amorous."

"I know which booth," she said, and picked up her coffee.

We sat with that for a moment. Outside the kitchen window the June morning was doing what June mornings do in Connecticut when they're behaving — the particular green of it, the light through the trees, the neighbor's dog conducting its investigation of the property line with professional thoroughness.

"Wayne Xavier," Cynthia said, mostly to herself. "You took him to the drive-in."

"He took me to the drive-in," I said. "The first time."

She looked up. "When was the first time."

"Summer of 1980," I said. "Norwalk Drive-In. You were fifteen."

She was quiet for a moment. I watched her go back — the filing system producing the folder, the folder containing a seventeen-year-old Lorri and a boy with a car and a Saturday night and a little sister who would have known about it and retained it and never said a word in forty-four years because it hadn't been relevant until now.

"I remember you going," she said.

"I thought you might."

"I don't remember him."

"You wouldn't," I said. "You were fifteen. He was auto shop. I was food trades. Different worlds."

"But the same cafeteria," she said.

"But the same cafeteria," I agreed.

She turned her mug in her hands — a slow rotation, the way she does when she's thinking through something she's not going to say directly. "And now he's coming to stay at the Butterfly Inn," she said. "For a weekend. In June."

"Yes."

"And you called me on a Saturday morning to tell me."

"Yes."

She looked at me over her glasses — the look that means she has a question she's decided not to ask yet. I know this look. I have known this look for fifty-nine years. It means she's chosen a different angle.

"What is he to you," she said.

There it was.

I looked at my coffee. I thought about the booth and the blouse and the craftsman's hands and the pause on the phone when I'd told him the kissing booth didn't have an upper limit. I thought about the Impala, which he'd bought junior year and kept because some things, once you have them, you don't let go of.

"I don't have a complete answer to that," I said.

Cynthia nodded as if this were the answer she'd expected, which it probably was. She didn't push. That's the thing about Cynthia — she probes sideways, but she knows when she's gotten what she came for. The question had landed. The fact that I didn't have an answer was itself the answer.

"I want to meet him," she said.

"I know you do."

"I want to meet the man who took my sister to the Norwalk Drive-In in 1980 and apparently made enough of an impression that she still remembers him in 2024."

"He had a red car," I said.

"They always have a red car," she said.

"He still has it."

She put down her mug. "Of course he does," she said, with the tone of a woman adding a data point to a file she's been building for some time. "Of course he still has the red car."

We had more coffee. We talked about other things — her work, the neighborhood, the particular lunacy of a case she was tracking at NMC involving a licensing dispute over a comic book character that had been in print since 1962. Cynthia can make IP law sound like a blood sport, which it apparently is. I listened and refilled her mug and thought about the weekend and what I still needed to think about.

At the door, her jacket on, she turned.

"Friday evening," she said. "At Amorous. Is there room for a little sister."

"There's always room," I said. "Come at seven. Meet him at the bar. Have one drink."

She smiled — the precise smile, the one that means she knows exactly what *one drink* means and is choosing not to say so. "One drink," she said.

"Cynthia."

"Yes."

"He doesn't lead with wit," I said. "Don't mistake that for something else."

She looked at me for a moment. Then: "Is he good to you."

"He's very good to me," I said.

She nodded. Filed it. Went down the walk to her car without looking back, which is how Cynthia leaves when she's satisfied.

I went back to the bistro table and finished my coffee alone and thought about a seventeen-year-old girl at the Norwalk Drive-In who hadn't been keeping careful records.

Some things you only understand later.

The Butterfly Inn

The Impala arrived at four o'clock.

Laura Palladino knew this because she was at the front desk when it pulled into the Butterfly Inn's parking lot — fire engine red, white top up against the June afternoon, the particular authority of a car that has been kept rather than collected. She watched it through the window for a moment before the driver's door opened.

Solid build. Salt-and-pepper hair, the natural curl of it. Work boots and clean dark jeans and a white dress shirt with the collar open — the outfit of a man who had thought about what he was wearing without making a production of having thought about it. He took a small bag from the trunk and came up the porch steps with the unhurried ease of a man who has been places before and knows how to arrive.

Laura had the reservation. *Xavier, Wayne. Friday through Sunday.* Stamford address. No notes.

She didn't need notes.

"Mr. Xavier," she said.

"Wayne," he said, and set his bag down and looked at the lobby the way people look at a room they've just decided they like — not admiringly, exactly, but with a quiet acknowledgment. The Butterfly Inn's lobby had that effect on people. Fourteen years of Laura's specific attention to what a room should feel like, which was: a house where someone actually lived, not a catalog of antique furniture arranged for effect.

She gave him the key — an actual key, not a card, because the Butterfly Inn had actual keys — and told him breakfast was between seven-thirty and nine-thirty, the wraparound porch was available any time, and if he needed anything the desk was staffed until ten.

"The parking lot," he said. "The Impala will be all right there."

"It'll be fine," she said. Then: "1960?"

He looked at her with the particular attention of a man recalibrating an assessment. "Yes."

"My father had a '58," she said. "Different car entirely. But the sound is similar." She paused. "You did the interior yourself."

A beat. "How'd you know."

"Because it's right," she said simply, and handed him his key.

He smiled — the slow kind, the kind that meant he was genuinely pleased and wasn't performing it — and picked up his bag and went upstairs.

Laura watched him go. Then she went back to what she'd been doing before the Impala pulled in, which was the week's bookings, and thought: *good for her.*

She didn't know specifically who *her* was. She had a reasonable hypothesis.

* * *

The Impala was still in the parking lot at seven when the restaurant two minutes up Main Street put Chet Baker on the back-bar and a woman in a gray hostess vest stood at the host stand and looked at the door.

Wayne Xavier arrived at Amorous at seven-fifteen. The desk at the Butterfly Inn noted the time because Laura Palladino noticed most things and wrote very few of them down and forgot almost none of them.

She went back to her bookings.

Good for her, she thought again.

The Booth

Cynthia arrived at seven on the dot, which for Cynthia meant she'd been in the parking lot since six fifty-five.

She came through the vestibule in dark trousers and a silk blouse the color of good Bordeaux and her reading glasses pushed up into her hair, which she does when she wants to look like she's not paying close attention and is in fact paying very close attention. I was at the host stand. She looked at me — at the vest, at the bowtie, at the quality of stillness I was giving the room — and said nothing, which from Cynthia is a form of comment.

"He's at the bar," I said.

"I see that," she said.

Wayne had arrived at six forty-five. Ginny had looked at him and said *I'm guessing an Old Fashioned would be agreeable*, and Wayne had said it would, and Ginny had built him one with the precision she brings to drinks she respects. He had been nursing it for fifteen minutes when Cynthia walked in — half a glass left, the orange peel still doing its work on the surface — and talking to Ginny with the ease of a man who is comfortable at bars and doesn't need to perform being comfortable at bars. Ginny was behind the counter doing what Ginny does — present, attentive, saying approximately nothing. They appeared to have reached a companionable understanding.

I walked Cynthia to the bar.

"Wayne Xavier," I said. "My sister Cynthia."

Wayne stood — not a production, just a man who stands when he's introduced to someone. He looked at Cynthia with the same steady warmth he brought to most things and extended his hand.

Cynthia took it and looked at him the way she looks at licensing agreements — completely, in one pass, missing nothing.

"You had a red car," she said.

Wayne looked at her. Then at me. Then back at Cynthia. "Still do," he said.

"Lorri said you were taller."

"Lorri was sixteen," he said.

Cynthia smiled — the precise one. "She was seventeen," she said. "I was fifteen. I remember the car."

"The Impala," Wayne said. "It's in the Butterfly Inn parking lot if you want to see it."

"I'll see it eventually," she said, and sat down at the bar with the settled authority of a woman who has gotten what she came for in the first thirty seconds and is now prepared to enjoy the rest of the evening.

* * *

Ginny poured Cynthia a glass without being asked — a Bordeaux, because Ginny had taken in the blouse and drawn her conclusions, which is what Ginny does. Cynthia registered the pour and said nothing, which meant she approved.

We sat at the bar, the three of us, and talked. About Wright Tech — the way the two buildings sat relative to each other, the smell of motor oil that had apparently permeated the auto shop wing so thoroughly that the food trades students two corridors over could tell you what they were working on by the afternoon air quality. About the cafeteria, which Wayne remembered as loud and Cynthia remembered as having an inexplicable devotion to a particular brand of chocolate pudding that had not appeared anywhere in the world since 1983.

"The Dover Drag Strip," I said, at some point.

Cynthia looked up.

"Summer of 1980," I said. "Wayne and Gia and I drove up through New Milford on Route 7 to Wingdale. New York side of the state line. Gia went to Stamford High — she had a friend who raced."

"She left us sitting in the stands," Wayne said, "while she found her way into the pit area."

"She came back an hour later," I said.

"With a smudge of grease," Wayne said, "that I decided not to ask about."

Cynthia looked at us with the expression of a woman for whom this explained a great deal about Gia Cummings, none of it surprising. "How many heats did you watch," she said.

"Four," I said.

"Before she disappeared."

"Before she disappeared," Wayne confirmed.

Cynthia nodded slowly, filing it. "That tracks," she said.

She stayed for one drink. She had said one drink and she meant one drink, which I had known and Wayne had not known but learned when she set down her glass at seven fifty-five and put on her jacket with the decisive motion of a woman who has completed what she came to do.

She kissed me on the cheek. She shook Wayne's hand again — a real handshake, both hands this time, the kind Cynthia reserves for people who have passed whatever internal assessment she runs on new arrivals.

"The car is red," she said to Wayne. "She said it was red. I remember that."

"It was always red," he said.

"Good," she said, as if this settled something. Then she walked through the dining room and through the vestibule and out into the June evening without looking back.

* * *

Ginny watched her go. She picked up Cynthia's glass and set it in the rack below the bar. She picked up a fresh glass and began to polish it.

She didn't say anything. She didn't need to.

The restaurant was settling into its Friday rhythm around us — the other tables doing what other tables do, the music from the back-bar cubbies threading through the room. Ginny had been moving the evening through the vocal jazz over the last hour, the slow recordings

I keep in the cubbies for the part of the night when the room asks for them. The candlelight doing the work that candlelight does when it's been given the right conditions. I looked at Wayne and Wayne looked at me and we both understood that the first part of the evening had concluded.

"Let's sit somewhere comfortable," I said.

I picked up both glasses and walked toward the corner.

* * *

He followed, and at the edge of the slatted screen I stopped and turned.

"Welcome back," I said, "to my kissing booth."

He looked at the booth — the red leather, the candle, the screen, the plant, the blinds drawn against Main Street — with the expression of a man for whom the memory of the last time he was here has been running on a quiet loop for three weeks.

"The upper limit," he said.

"There isn't one," I said. "I mentioned that."

"You mentioned that," he agreed.

"Come in," I said. "Before the candle burns down."

* * *

I gestured for him to slide in first. He did. I settled close — the way you settle when close is the point — and his arm went around my shoulders with the ease of a man who has been thinking about exactly this and is relieved to discover the reality matches the thought.

The room moved around us at its own pace. Ginny behind the bar, in the amber light, doing what she always does. The music unhurried. The other tables in their own worlds.

He kissed me. Not a question, not yet a destination — the first kiss of an evening, the one that says *here we are*. Warm and certain. I kissed him back. The first kiss of an evening always says yes back.

We were on the second kiss when Ginny arrived with the plates.

She came around the slatted screen with two small plates and a carafe of water and two glasses balanced on a small tray, set the tray down on the edge of the table, and began arranging.

"Drinks okay?" she said.

"Water's okay for now," I said.

She placed the first plate — prosciutto wrapped around figs, small, six pieces, glossy. She placed the second — crostini with ricotta and truffle honey, four pieces, a little drizzle on each. She poured the water into both glasses.

Then she stepped around to the side of the booth, set her hand on the rim of the heavy ceramic pot, and slid it — slowly, easily, the slippery holder doing its quiet work — until the plant blocked the opening between the slatted screen and the edge of the booth.

"I'll give you a little privacy," she said.

Wayne laughed — low and pleased, the laugh of a man hearing a piece of architecture explain itself. "That's a good sign," he said.

Ginny did not respond. She walked back to the bar.

I looked at Wayne. "Two stage directions," I said. "She just gave us two."

"I noticed both."

"The plant slides out, the privacy begins. The plant slides back, the privacy ends."

"And how does the plant slide back."

"I slide it," I said. "When I'm ready."

Wayne considered this. "An elegant system."

"I designed it," I said.

"Of course you did."

* * *

We ate.

The figs first. I picked one up and looked at it and looked at Wayne and bit it in half — the warm sweet inside the salt of the prosciutto, the give of it, the small bright flare of it on the tongue. Wayne watched me eat it and then picked one up and did the same, and there was honey or something like honey on his lower lip when he looked at me, and I leaned in and licked it off, and he laughed — surprised — and kissed me, and there was a little bit of fig somewhere in that kiss and neither of us minded.

"This is going to be a messy evening," he said.

"I'm counting on it," I said.

He picked up a crostini and held it out to me. I took the bite he offered me. Ricotta and truffle honey and the crunch of the toast and his thumb at the corner of my mouth catching what fell.

"You missed some," he said.

"I'm sure I did."

He leaned in and kissed the corner of my mouth where the honey had been and then my mouth fully and the kiss carried the truffle honey between us — sweet, animal, faintly savage. His tongue found mine and I let it.

I sat back a little. "You're going to be unbearable at the next two of these."

"Two of what."

"Plates."

"There's another plate?"

"There's another plate," I said. "Ginny paces these."

"How many plates are there."

"You'll find out."

"Mysterious."

"I'm a mysterious woman."

"You're a planner."

"I'm a planner who's also unpredictable," I said. "It's a range."

He kissed me again. Long. The kind of kiss where you stop tracking time because time has agreed to stop tracking you.

* * *

The small low whistle came from the edge of the slatted screen — two notes, falling, the wry tune of a woman pretending not to know what she was interrupting.

A brief pause.

Ginny's hand appeared on the rim of the plant's pot and pulled it aside in one easy motion, the slippery holder doing its work. She stepped through with the second plate balanced on a small tray, looked once at the table, looked once at us, and said *hey lovebirds* in the tone of a woman pronouncing an accurate observation.

She set down the new plate — marcona almonds and a few good olives and two thin slices of something hard and pale that I recognized as the manchego Martin had been saving for something worth saving for. She took the empty fig plate. She did not take the crostini plate; there were still two crostini on it and Ginny knew this and left them.

On her way out she pulled the plant closed behind her.

"Lovebirds," Wayne said.

"Aren't we?" I said.

"I'm being categorized."

"You're being correctly categorized."

"That's worse."

"It is somewhat worse," I agreed.

He thought about something.

"She has a whistle."

"She developed it. Organically."

"C'mon. I bet you two practiced this over tequila."

I smiled.

"Is there a manual for this place?"

"No."

"There should be."

I leaned in to kiss him and his right hand came up to my face — palm against my cheek, thumb along my jaw, the patient warm specificity of a man learning a face he intends to know — and held me there, and kissed me back, slowly, the kind of kiss that establishes that everything happening from here will be unhurried.

When we eased apart he picked up an almond and placed it carefully between my lips. I bit into it and felt his thumb still at my mouth and the salt of the almond and the warmth of him and the fact that the restaurant was nearly empty around us and that none of it was relevant.

We ate the second plate slowly. Olive between kisses. Almond between kisses. The manchego we ate with our fingers and Wayne's left hand stayed where it was, around my shoulders, and his right hand moved between the plate and my mouth and my face and my mouth again. When he kissed me there was salt and the slow turn of his tongue and the warmth of an evening that was doing what it had been designed to do.

His hand came to rest, at some point, against the front of my vest. Open palm. Present. Not pressing. Just *there,* against the wool, where it had every reason to be and was not yet doing what it had come to do.

I noticed.

He noticed me noticing.

Neither of us said anything about it.

We kept kissing. His tongue moving in mine, mine answering, the slow careful exchange that two adults conduct when they have all the time in the world and have decided to spend it on this. His hand on the vest, patient, warm, *waiting.*

The waiting was its own thing. The waiting was, I realized, the entire point.

* * *

I sat back, finally, just enough to look at him.

His hair slightly disordered. His mouth flushed. His eyes warm and steady and entirely on me.

"Coffee soon," I said.

"Not yet."

"No. Not yet."

"Good," he said.

"I want a Drambuie first."

He thought about that. "I don't think I've had one."

"You'll like this."

"You're telling me what I'll like."

"I'm correct."

"I'm aware."

I leaned slightly out of the booth and made eye contact with Ginny across the room — one look, two seconds, the small wave of a woman summoning her bartender — and she registered it and nodded and went to work.

She came back fairly quickly, which is what Ginny does when she's been signaled rather than guessed at. She brought two small glasses of Drambuie on a small tray. She set them on the table. She checked the water carafe. She poured a little more into each glass.

"You're set on water," she said.

"We are."

She did not say anything else. She stepped around to the side of the booth and slid the plant back into its blocking position — the same easy slide, the slippery holder doing its work, the privacy sealed.

She walked away.

* * *

Wayne picked up his Drambuie. He looked at it — the amber, the heather-honey scent — and took a small sip.

He looked at me.

"You were right," he said.

"I know."

"That's very good."

"Wait until you taste it on me."

He looked at me.

I took a small sip of mine and leaned in and kissed him — slowly, the Drambuie passing between us, the heather and honey and Scotch warming everything they touched. His tongue found the sweetness and stayed there. He licked my lower lip clean. I returned the favor. We tasted the same and the tasting was its own pleasure — the slow exchange of a thing better shared than swallowed.

"That's a different drink now," he said.

"It is a different drink."

"I want some more of that drink."

"There's a lot more of that drink."

* * *

The track ended. A new one began — slower, a piano holding a few opening chords. Then a baritone voice settled into the room over a tenor saxophone, both of them unhurried, both of them deep enough to be felt as much as heard.

Wayne tilted his head slightly. He listened for a few bars.

"Lorri."

"Mm."

"You set this to music."

"I set it to music."

"You didn't need to add music."

"Didn't I."

"I was already fully engaged."

I kissed him.

* * *

I reached for the vest buttons.

Four of them.

I was looking at Wayne the whole time. He was looking back. Neither of us spoke. My fingers were unhurried and entirely competent, which is how my fingers tend to be when I have decided what they are doing.

I undid the first. Then the second. Then the third. Then the fourth.

I did not move the vest.

The vest moved itself — fell open along the line of buttons because what was beneath had been engineered to push it open. The two halves of dark wool slid apart and settled at my sides and the white blouse appeared in the candlelight, fitted, full, the architecture beneath it pushing the front of the blouse forward into the space between us.

I looked at Wayne.

He was looking at my face. Then at my chest. Then back at my face.

I smiled.

The smile became, by degrees, a smirk — the smirk of a woman who had constructed this specific moment, knew exactly what she had constructed, and was watching the construction land.

Wayne saw the smirk.

"May I," he said.

"Yes," I said. "Slowly."

* * *

He was slow.

The first button, then a pause. The candlelight finding the cotton beneath. Then the second — unhurried, deliberate. The third. The blouse opened.

And there was the bra — the custom one from White Street in Danbury, the smooth white cups, the precise engineering of a thing built to specification by someone who understood the assignment. Not a suggestion. A structure. A presence. Something that had been there all evening underneath the blouse underneath the vest, waiting.

Wayne looked at it.

The craftsman's pause — taking in the whole of something before he touches it. Then his right hand settled against the cup. Gently. The palm warm through the smooth white fabric, learning what was there. He kissed me and his hand moved — slowly, with the deliberate attention of a man who understands that this is the destination — pressing, the smooth white fabric shifting against what it contained.

Then his hand opened fully and my breast settled into his palm — the full warm weight of it sliding against his hand — and his fingers closed around it with the instinct of a man who has been given something and knows it.

He held it. He kissed me. His left arm stayed where it always was, steady around my shoulders, drawing me in. His right hand learned what it held and I felt the warmth of it travel from that specific geography outward in every direction at once.

We kissed. Long minutes of it. His tongue finding mine and my tongue answering, the communication channel open between us while his hand held and pressed and explored with the patience of a craftsman who has been given good material and all the time he needs. One side and then the other — the cup presenting each in its own turn, smooth and warm and full.

* * *

I shifted.

I'd been slouching into him for I don't know how long, and my spine had finally decided to register an opinion. I sat back against the booth and stretched a little — small, just enough to undo what had been collecting between my shoulder blades.

"I'm slouching," I said.

"You're slouching," he agreed.

"I'm getting old."

"You're remarkably preserved."

"That's the wrong word."

"It's the word I have."

"Try harder."

"I'll work on it."

He kissed my temple. Then the corner of my jaw. His right hand left where it had been and moved up to the back of my neck — the slow careful pressure of a man whose hands knew where tension lives — and worked the muscle there. His left arm stayed where it was. The booth held us both. The Hartman voice continued to settle over the saxophone like something poured.

I closed my eyes.

"You're good at that," I said.

"I have hands."

"You have hands."

"They have opinions."

"They have a lot of opinions."

He kissed the side of my throat, then back to my mouth, slowly, his hand still working at the base of my neck. The kiss was quieter than the kisses before it — companionable, warm, two people who had been at this long enough that the urgency had pooled and settled into something more sustained. I took a slow sip of my Drambuie and set the glass back down and leaned into his hand on my neck.

"This is good too," I said.

"This is part of it."

"Mm."

"You're going to be sore tomorrow," he said.

"Thoroughly," I said.

He laughed against my throat — a small low laugh, the kind that doesn't need to be heard by anyone else to be a laugh.

"This is technically our fourth date," he said. "If you include Norwalk."

"You're counting the drive-in as a date."

"It counted."

"Forty-six years between dates one and two."

"I'm patient."

"Do you think I'm too easy?"

He looked at me. The smile lines deep. The eyes warm.

"You're a boy's fantasy come true," he said.

And then his hand moved from my neck back down across my shoulder and his right hand returned slowly, by degrees, to where it had been before, finding the cup again, finding what was waiting inside it, settling.

His palm closed around what was inside the cup and stayed there. He kissed me — long and unhurried, the way the evening had been teaching him to kiss — while his hand learned again what it had learned before. The cup shifting smoothly against my skin under his palm. The warmth of his hand traveling outward in the way it always traveled outward.

I arched slightly into his hand. I could not help it and did not try.

"We're canoodling," I said, when I'd caught my breath.

He looked at me — flushed, warm, the smile lines deep around his eyes.

"That's what this is called," I said.

He considered this with the seriousness it deserved. "Canoodling," he said.

"Canoodling," I confirmed. "Remember the word. You'll need it."

"Ummm."

"What."

"Look."

"What."

"You're remarkably well constructed."

"You're measuring them."

"I'm appreciating them."

"You're measuring them," I said. "It's fine. They were built to be measured."

He laughed — low, against my mouth — and kissed me again, his hand warm and unhurried where it was, and I thought: *yes. Exactly this. This is the word for it.*

He sipped his Drambuie. He kissed me. I sipped mine. He kissed me. We traded sips. We traded kisses. His hand stayed where it had been welcomed and continued the patient work of getting acquainted with what it had been given. The candle burned down by some quantity I did not measure. The restaurant continued to do whatever it was doing on the other side of the slatted screen and the slid plant and the drawn blinds. None of it was our concern.

* * *

I lost track of how long.

I did not lose track of him. I was entirely present in every minute of it — his hand, his mouth, his tongue, the weight of his arm around my shoulders, the warm liqueur in our mouths, the smooth fabric shifting between his palm and my skin. I knew where every part of him was, every minute of it, and where every part of me was, and what we were doing, and what we had decided not to do, and that the decision itself was part of the heat.

When at some point I sat back and looked at him I saw a man who had been somewhere very specific and was now slowly coming back from it.

"Coffee," I said.

"Coffee," he agreed.

I buttoned the blouse. Slowly. He watched me do it the way he had watched me open the vest — steadily, with the expression of a man who has been given something to think about and is already thinking about it. I did not button the vest. I left it open.

I leaned out of the booth and stood and took the two steps to the side of the plant and slid it back to where it had started, beside the booth, out of the way.

I sat down again. I picked up my Drambuie. There was a swallow left. I drank it slowly.

* * *

Ginny appeared within a minute.

She brought a small tray with two cups of coffee, cream, sugar, and the Drambuie bottle. She set everything down on the table. She took the empty Drambuie glasses from before and the second plate. She refilled the water glasses once before she went.

"I'll leave the bottle," she said.

"Yes," I said. "Good."

"Anything else?"

"Not yet."

She nodded once and went back to the bar.

* * *

Wayne picked up the bottle and added a small measure to my coffee. Then to his. He stirred neither of them. He set the bottle down between us.

We sat in the booth and drank our coffee.

We did not talk for a while. We did not need to. He sipped his coffee and looked at me with the warm steady expression of a man who had been given an evening and had spent it inside the evening and was now slowly stepping outside it to look at the shape of what he had been given. I drank mine and watched him do this and let him do it without comment.

After a while: "Tomorrow," he said.

"Tomorrow."

"Breakfast at the inn?"

"I'll come find you."

"I assumed."

"You assume well."

"I'm good at assuming. It's adjacent to planning."

He sipped his coffee. He looked at me.

"You designed an entire evening."

"I designed an entire evening."

"Including the plant."

"Including the plant."

"Including Ginny."

"Ginny isn't designed. Ginny is recruited."

"Recruited."

"Long ago," I said. "And once."

He picked up the bottle and added a little more to his cup. He held it out to me. I held my cup out to him and he poured.

"It worked," he said.

"I know," I said.

"All of it."

"All of it."

He set the bottle down and reached for my hand on the table and held it. The candle burned down a little further. The coffee warmed our hands and our throats and the part of the evening that needed to come down to ground.

* * *

When he stood up to leave he stood the way Wayne stands — not a production, just a man rising from a booth at the end of an evening. He looked at me for a long moment.

"Tomorrow," he said.

"Tomorrow."

We kissed goodbye in the vestibule — one, and another, and a third that made the first two seem like a preamble — and I stood in the doorway and watched him walk up Main Street toward the Butterfly Inn in the June night, his hands in his pockets, unhurried.

I went back inside.

The restaurant was empty. Ginny was behind the bar, back to the room. The record had finished. The back-bar sat in its amber shadow, the VU meters glowing their quiet blue-green.

I walked to the corner booth and sat in it alone.

The candle still lit. The seat warm where he'd been. The bowtie on the table where I'd left it.

I sat in the booth I had built and thought about what had happened in it tonight — not the Electrician, last November, when the booth had simply been the place we ended up. Tonight I had put Wayne here on purpose. I had worn this vest on purpose. I had waited at the first button on purpose, and he had asked the right question, and the blouse had opened, and the bra had been there, and his hand had found it with the care of a craftsman approaching material he respects.

It had worked. All of it had worked.

Ginny walked from the bar to the booth one more time. She stood at the edge of the slatted screen and looked at me sitting alone with the candle and the bowtie and whatever was on my face.

One second.

"Tomorrow," she said.

I looked at her.

"He'll be back tomorrow," she said. Not a question.

"Yes," I said.

She nodded. Went back to the bar.

I blew out the candle. Put on my coat. Drove home to Middlebury with the window down, the June air coming through warm and clean, the river valley dark on either side of the road.

Some things, once you've found them, you don't let go of.

I was beginning to understand that this applied in both directions.

Saturday Morning

I arrived at the Butterfly Inn at eight-fifteen on Saturday morning with the particular energy of a woman who has slept well and knows why.

The wraparound porch was empty at that hour except for a pair of rocking chairs that had clearly been placed by someone who understood what a June morning in Connecticut deserves. The hydrangeas along the porch rail were doing what hydrangeas do in June, which is everything, all at once, without apology. I stood for a moment before going in and thought that Laura Palladino had built something worth building.

Then I went inside.

* * *

The breakfast room was off the lobby — four tables, white linen, a sideboard with coffee and fruit and the particular smell of something baking that had been in the oven since before I woke up. Wayne was at the table by the window with a cup of coffee and the expression of a man who has slept well and is comfortable not knowing what comes next.

He looked up when I came in.

"You're here," he said.

"I'm here," I said. "Move over."

He moved over. I sat down and took his coffee and drank from it and handed it back and he accepted this without comment, which was the right response.

Laura Palladino appeared from the kitchen doorway with a coffee pot and the focused warmth of a woman who runs her own room and knows exactly what's in it. She looked at me — one second, the full assessment — and then she smiled.

"You must be Lorri," she said.

"I must be," I said. "You're Laura."

"I've been meaning to come to Amorous since you opened," she said, pouring my coffee.

"The ribbon cutting was in Voices," I said. "You had no excuse."

"I had every excuse," she said. "I have an inn. Excuses are the main product." She set the pot down and looked between us with the particular warmth of a woman who has already filed everything she needs to file and is now simply enjoying the morning. "Breakfast is whatever you'd like. Aurora made scones."

"Aurora is home?" I said.

"Home for the weekend." She tilted her head toward the kitchen. "She'll be devastated she missed the introduction."

"There will be other mornings," I said.

Laura smiled — the quick one, the one that meant she had noted this and intended to remember it — and went back to the kitchen.

* * *

Wayne watched her go. "You know her," he said.

"I just met her," I said.

"You talk like you know her."

"We're both women who built something on Main Street," I said. "There's a shorthand."

He considered this with the equanimity of a man who accepts that there are frequencies he doesn't receive. "She knew about the car," he said.

"She would," I said. "She notices things."

"Like Ginny."

I looked at him. "A little like Ginny," I said. "Different register. Ginny gives you one word. Laura gives you four sentences that add up to the same thing."

He nodded slowly, adding this to whatever internal file he kept on the women in Lorri Oliver's orbit, which was apparently a growing file. "The Butterfly Inn," he said. "You told me it was like Gilmore Girls."

"It is like Gilmore Girls."

"You're going to have to explain that," he said. "You mentioned it on the phone and I looked it up and then I had more questions."

I looked at him. "You looked it up."

"I looked it up," he said, without embarrassment. "Seven seasons. There's a lot of it."

"There's a lot of it," I agreed. I wrapped both hands around my coffee and thought about where to begin with a man who had spent an evening researching a television program because a woman on the phone had mentioned it. "All right," I said. "Gilmore Girls. There's a town called Stars Hollow. Small, preserved, everyone knows everyone. The kind of town that resists the twenty-first century on principle."

"Thornbury," he said.

"Thornbury," I agreed. "There's an inn in Stars Hollow called the Dragonfly Inn. The owner runs it with her daughter. Warm, quick, talks faster than most people think. Knows every guest's name before they've unpacked."

Wayne looked toward the kitchen door.

"Yes," I said. "Exactly."

"And Luke," he said. "The coffee shop."

"Luke's Diner," I said. "He's there every morning. He's been there every morning for years. He and the inn owner have a — complicated history."

"Complicated how."

"The kind of complicated," I said, "that takes seven seasons to resolve."

Wayne was quiet for a moment. He looked at his coffee. He looked at the kitchen door. He looked at me with the expression of a man arriving at a conclusion he hadn't expected to arrive at when he woke up this morning. "That's why you said I could be Luke," he said.

"That's why I said you could be Luke," I said.

"Because I keep coming back."

"Because," I said, "you keep coming back."

He sat with this. Outside the window the June morning was doing its best work — the hydrangeas, the porch light still on from the night before, a cardinal in the maple that had apparently claimed the Butterfly Inn's front yard as its personal territory and was conducting its affairs accordingly.

"I've been thinking about it," he said.

I looked at him.

"Relocating," he said. "The business. There's a shop in Woodbury — space above it. I've been looking at it for a few months."

The fork trembled.

I did not pick it up. I set my coffee down and looked at the cardinal in the maple and thought about a man who bought a car junior year and kept it because some things, once you have them, you don't let go of. I thought about seven seasons of complicated history and a diner that was there every morning.

"Woodbury," I said.

"Five minutes from Thornbury," he said.

"I know where Woodbury is," I said.

He smiled — the slow kind. "I thought you might," he said.

* * *

Laura came back with the scones and her daughter Aurora behind her — twenty years old, her mother's eyes, a dish towel over one shoulder and the slightly flustered energy of someone who had been told there were guests and had come to see for herself. She looked at me and looked at Wayne and looked at her mother with a question she did not ask.

Laura set the scones down. "Lorri owns Amorous," she said to Aurora. "The restaurant on Main Street."

"I've heard about it," Aurora said. "I've been trying to get Mom to go."

"I've been trying to get your mother to go," I said. "We've both been failing."

"We'll go," Laura said, to the room generally, in the tone of a woman making a promise she intends to keep on her own schedule.

Aurora sat down at the edge of the table with the comfort of a girl who grew up in this room and has never needed an invitation. She looked at Wayne with the frank assessment of someone raised by a woman who notices things. "Is that your Impala in the parking lot," she said.

"It is," Wayne said.

"1960?"

"Yes."

"My grandmother had a photograph of one," she said. "Same color. She always said it was the best-looking car ever made."

"She wasn't wrong," Wayne said.

Aurora smiled — her mother's smile, quicker — and got up and went back to the kitchen with the dish towel and whatever else she'd come to see.

Laura watched her go. Then she looked at me with the expression of a woman who has just watched a Saturday morning arrange itself into something worth remembering.

"More coffee," she said, and poured it without waiting for an answer.

* * *

We sat at the Butterfly Inn until ten o'clock. We ate the scones, which were very good, and drank the coffee, which was excellent, and talked about Thornbury and Woodbury and the particular quality of the WoodThorn Corridor in June when the road runs through the river valley and the light comes through the trees at an angle that makes you understand why people write poems about Connecticut. Laura joined us twice more and each time stayed long enough to say one thing that landed and then returned to whatever required her attention, which was either the actual operation of an inn or a considered performance of it — I was not sure which and suspected the distinction didn't matter.

At ten o'clock Wayne said: "The Impala has the top down."

"Does it," I said.

"It does," he said. "I put it down this morning."

"That was optimistic of you," I said.

"I'm an optimistic man," he said.

I looked at him across the white linen and the coffee cups and the crumbs of Aurora's scones and thought about Woodbury. Five minutes from Thornbury. A shop with a space above it.

"There's an amusement park," I said. "Quassy. It's been there since 1952. Twenty minutes from here."

He looked at me. "You're suggesting we go to an amusement park."

"I'm observing that there's an amusement park," I said, "and that you have a convertible and that the weather is holding."

The pause this time was very short.

"Let's go," he said.

* * *

Laura was at the desk when we came through the lobby. She looked at us — the two of us, the morning behind us, whatever was on our faces — and said nothing useful, which was exactly right.

At the door I turned. "Amorous," I said. "Thursday through Monday. Come any evening."

"I'll come," she said. "I'll bring Aurora."

"Bring Aurora," I said.

She smiled. We went out onto the porch and down the steps and into the June morning where the Impala was waiting in the parking lot with the top down, fire engine red in the Saturday sun, the red leather interior bright and warm.

Wayne opened the door. I got in.

Some mornings arrange themselves, I thought. You just have to show up for them.

Quassy

Quassy Amusement Park sits on the shore of Lake Quassapaug in Middlebury, and has been sitting there since 1908, when it was the last stop on the trolley line out of Waterbury. Factory families would ride out on a Saturday with picnic baskets and spend the day on the lake. The trolley is gone. The park is not. The Frantzis family has run it for generations and has declined, at every opportunity, to make it into something it isn't. It is not a theme park. It is not a resort. It is an amusement park — rides and games and a midway and a lake and a snack bar that still sells what snack bars are supposed to sell.

We paid at the gate and walked in and became part of it.

* * *

The Impala had attracted attention on Route 64 — it always does, Wayne had explained, which is why he takes the back roads when he can and the main roads when he can't and has made his peace with both. A red 1960 convertible with the top down on a Saturday in June is not a thing that passes unnoticed, which Wayne neither courts nor avoids. He simply drives it and lets the car be what it is.

In the Quassy parking lot a boy of approximately eight had stood next to it for a full minute before his father collected him. Wayne had answered three questions about the engine with the patience and brevity of a man who has answered these questions ten thousand times and found them worth answering every time.

I watched him do this and thought: *this is what he's like.*

* * *

We walked the midway. Fried dough and something from the snack bar that smelled like summer and the particular sound of a carousel that has been playing the same songs for seventy years and has no intention of changing its repertoire. Children in every direction, moving at the speed of children who have been given permission to run.

Wayne bought two tickets for the Ferris wheel without discussing it.

"The Ferris wheel," I said.

"The Ferris wheel," he said.

"That was decisive."

"I'm a decisive man," he said, and handed me a ticket.

* * *

The Ferris wheel at Quassy is not a modern thing — not the kind that moves continuously, loading passengers in a smooth rotation. It stops. It loads a car, stops, loads the next, stops again, working its way around in increments until everyone is seated and the whole wheel turns together. This means that if you are in the last car to be loaded, you spend the loading time at the top.

We were in the last car.

The attendant — sixteen years old, the summer job visible in his posture — latched the bar across our laps and moved to the next station and we rose, incrementally, stop by stop, as the cars below us filled. The lake came into view. Then the tree line. Then the particular blue of a Connecticut June sky that is different from the blue of any other month and cannot be adequately described to someone who has not seen it.

We stopped at the top.

Below us, Quassy went about its business — the carousel still playing, the midway still moving, the snack bar still fragrant. None of it was paying attention to the top of the Ferris wheel. Nobody ever pays attention to the top of the Ferris wheel.

Wayne looked at the lake. I looked at Wayne.

"You planned this," he said.

"I observed that there was a Ferris wheel," I said, "and that you had a ticket."

He turned to look at me — the steady warmth of him, the smile lines, the salt-and-pepper in the June light — and kissed me.

Not tentative. Not a question. His mouth warm and certain against mine, his arm along the back of the car finding my shoulders, the particular ease of a man who has been thinking about kissing this woman since he woke up this morning and is relieved to have found the right moment for it.

I kissed him back and felt the warmth of it and the height of it simultaneously — the lake below and the blue above and the carousel playing its seventy-year-old song and the fact of being sixty years old at the top of a Ferris wheel in June being kissed by a man who drove from Stamford in a red convertible because some things, once you've found them, you don't let go of.

The wheel began to move.

We broke apart as the car descended — unhurried, neither of us in any particular rush to stop being where we were. Below us the park reassembled itself, the midway and the children and the snack bar coming back into range.

"The Norwalk Drive-In," Wayne said. "1980."

"Yes," I said.

"We didn't have a Ferris wheel."

"No," I said. "We didn't."

"Better," he said.

"Much better," I said. "We were wasted on being seventeen."

He laughed — low and warm and genuine — and kept his arm around my shoulders as the car descended through the summer air toward the ground, the lake still blue behind us, the carousel still playing, Quassy still going about its seventy-year-old business without comment.

* * *

We stayed another hour. We walked the midway and Wayne won something at the ring toss — a small stuffed bear, orange, the kind of prize that exists only at midways and serves no purpose whatsoever — and handed it to me with the solemnity of a man presenting something of value.

I accepted it with equivalent solemnity.

"I'll put it at the host stand," I said.

"Don't do that," he said.

"I'll put it in the office," I said.

"Better," he said.

We had fried dough at a picnic table near the lake and watched the paddle boats and talked about nothing in particular, which is its own kind of luxury. The orange bear sat on the table between us. A child at the next table regarded it with professional assessment and moved on.

At two o'clock we walked back to the Impala. The parking lot had filled and the Impala had acquired a small audience — two men in their fifties circling it with the reverence of people who remember when cars like this were new. Wayne answered their questions with the same patience and brevity he'd given the eight-year-old, and they thanked him and went back to their own cars, which were sensible and uninteresting and had not been kept since 1980.

I got in. Wayne got in. The engine turned over with the sound that had been turning heads on Route 64 since before either of us was born.

"Sunday," Wayne said.

"Sunday," I agreed.

"What's Sunday."

I thought about it. "Sunday," I said, "is whatever we decide it is."

He put the Impala in gear and we pulled out of the Quassy parking lot into the Saturday afternoon and drove back through Middlebury toward Thornbury with the top down and the June air moving through the car and the orange bear wedged between the seat and the door, going wherever we were going, which was enough.

Thornbury

Richard set his coffee down the way Richard does everything — without ceremony, without noise.

"Cookie Magnifico has applied to the Merchants Association," he said.

I looked at him.

"Cookie Magnifico," I said.

"That's the name on the application."

Behind the bar, Ginny picked up a glass.

I had known, in the abstract way you know things about a town you've lived adjacent to for three years, that Thornbury had a Cookie Magnifico. She ran the gift shop on Elm that sold wind chimes and what I can only describe as aggressively seasonal wreaths. She was not, to my knowledge, a merchant in any sense that required association. She was more of a presence. A civic weather system.

"Is Magnifico her — "

"Married name," Richard said. "Forty years."

I considered this. The lunch crowd had thinned to nothing and the room was doing its afternoon thing, settling into its own light. The pink held. It always holds.

"What does the application say? Under business description."

Richard reached into his jacket — he'd actually brought the paper — and read: "Purveyor of curated gifts, seasonal décor, and handcrafted items of local significance."

"Wind chimes," I said.

"Wind chimes," he agreed.

He set the application down and folded his hands in the way that meant there was more.

"I looked her up on the Secretary of State website," he said. "Cookie is her actual name. But her middle name —" He paused. Richard never pauses. "Buttkiss."

I put my cup down.

"Cookie Buttkiss Magnifico," I said.

"On her birth certificate and everything."

The room did not change. The light held its pink. Somewhere behind me I heard Ginny set a glass down with a precision that suggested she was now paying closer attention.

I thought about Pat Devereaux at the Senior Center folding table, calling roll with the nameplate in front of her. I had already been picturing Pat's face for Magnifico. That had seemed like enough. That had seemed like the whole joke.

It was not the whole joke.

"She married a Magnifico," I said, mostly to myself.

"She did."

"Knowing."

"Presumably."

There is a kind of courage that doesn't get enough credit. The courage of a woman named Cookie Buttkiss who looks at a man named Magnifico and thinks: *yes. This is my way out.* Who walks toward that name with intention and gratitude and never looks back. Who builds a life, opens a shop, sells wind chimes, and one day applies to the Merchants Association under the full, magnificent weight of what she has become.

I picked up my coffee.

"Welcome her warmly," I said.

"Already drafted the letter," Richard said.

"Make sure Pat reads the full name at roll call."

Richard looked at me. "The bylaws require it anyway."

A beat.

"Even better," I said.

From the end of the bar, without looking up, Ginny said: "Nameplate's going to be a conversation piece."

It was the longest thing she'd said all afternoon.

Roll Call

The Thornbury Senior Center smelled the way civic spaces smell when they've been used well for a long time — floor wax and institutional coffee and the particular staleness of folded metal chairs that have held a thousand different conversations and retained the warmth of none of them individually and all of them collectively.

Pat Devereaux was already at the table when I arrived.

This is the nature of Pat Devereaux. She is always already at the table. I have attended four Merchants Association meetings in this room and Pat has been at the table before every one of them, her reading glasses on, the roster in front of her, the particular stillness of a woman who considers arriving on time a form of lateness.

She looked up when I came in. "Lorri."

"Pat."

"Richard's already here," she said, and returned to the roster.

Richard was at the coffee station doing what Richard does at coffee stations — assessing the situation with the calm resignation of a man who has made peace with institutional coffee because the alternative is no coffee and the alternative is unacceptable.

We found seats. Tom Caulder arrived, then Caroline Fitch with her precise timing, then the others in the usual order. The room filled with the particular sound of a small-town civic meeting beginning — chairs scraping, coffee cups settling, the low-register murmur of people who see each other regularly in professional capacity and have developed the shorthand of it.

Pat put on her reading glasses.

"I'll call the roll," she said. "And we have one new member applicant for introduction this evening."

She read the names in alphabetical order — the merchants of Thornbury, the civic fabric of a town that had worked very hard to remain the kind of town worth working hard for. She read each name with the flat precision of a woman for whom names are data, not commentary.

She reached the B's.

"Celeste Beaumont," she said. The room did not react. Pat moved on.

She reached the M's.

She paused — not long, barely a beat, the pause of a woman who has looked at this name on the roster twice and has decided she will read it exactly as written because the bylaws require it and because she is Pat Devereaux and she does not editorialize.

"Cookie Buttkiss Magnifico," she said.

From the far end of the table, a hand went up.

She was sixty-ish, round-faced, wearing a cardigan the color of a harvest moon with a small ceramic pumpkin pinned to the lapel that suggested we were approximately three weeks into her seasonal décor cycle and she was committed to it. She had the expression of a woman who has heard her name read aloud in public many times and has developed, across those many times, the serene equanimity of someone who knows exactly who she is and has made her peace with all of it.

Her nameplate read: *COOKIE B. MAGNIFICO.*

I looked at the nameplate. I looked at Cookie Buttkiss Magnifico. I looked at Richard, who was looking at his coffee with the focused attention of a man who has decided his coffee requires his complete concentration for the next several seconds.

"Welcome," Pat said, and moved to the next item on the agenda.

* * *

Afterward, in the parking lot, Richard fell into step beside me.

"The nameplate," he said.

"I saw it."

"She brought it herself," he said. "It was in her bag."

I thought about a woman who carries her own nameplate to her first Merchants Association meeting. Who has it made in advance — the full

B. included, neither hiding it nor announcing it, simply presenting it as the fact it is. Who sets it in front of her at the table with the same ease she'd hang a wind chime.

"Of course she did," I said.

Richard said nothing. He had the expression he reserves for moments when Lorri has summarized a situation correctly and further comment would diminish it.

We walked to our cars through the October evening. Somewhere on Main Street a wind chime was doing its work in the autumn air, though that may have been my imagination.

The Association

Tom Caulder arrived on a Tuesday afternoon in July with a canvas tote bag, a manila folder, and the expression of a man who has been meaning to do this for eighteen months and has finally run out of reasons not to.

Richard had mentioned him — peripherally, the way Richard mentions things he considers my decision. *Tom Caulder from the Merchants Association. He'll come by eventually.* This had been in the spring, and eventually had turned out to be July, which in Tom's defense was faster than some eventuallys I had encountered.

He was sixty-ish, trim, a blue oxford shirt with the sleeves rolled to the elbow — the uniform of a man who takes civic responsibility seriously without being solemn about it. He came through the vestibule at three o'clock on a Tuesday when Amorous was between its afternoon prep and its evening service and the dining room had the particular quality of a room that knows what it's for and is resting before it does it again.

I was at the host stand. Ginny was behind the bar doing something with the inventory that she prefers to do without being observed.

"Lorri Oliver," he said, and extended his hand. "Tom Caulder. Thornbury Merchants Association."

"I know who you are," I said, and shook it. "Richard said you'd come by."

"Richard said you'd be expecting me."

"Richard was optimistic," I said. "Come in. Sit at the bar."

* * *

Ginny poured him a sparkling water without being asked and went back to her inventory with the serene efficiency of a woman who has decided this conversation doesn't require her participation and is correct.

Tom put the manila folder on the bar and looked at the room — the back-bar, the vinyl cubbies, the VU meters dark at this hour, the pendant lights off and the afternoon coming through the blinds in the particular slanted way it does at three o'clock. He looked at it the way people look at Amorous when they're seeing it for the first time without the evening's atmosphere to carry them — seeing the bones of it, the actual thing Lorri and Richard had built.

"I was at the ribbon cutting," he said.

"I remember," I said.

"April 2023." He looked at the back-bar. "It looked different then."

"It looked the same," I said. "You're looking at it differently."

He considered this and seemed to find it accurate. "Eighteen months," he said. "You've been open eighteen months and we haven't gotten you into the Association."

"I've been busy," I said.

"I know you have," he said. "That's actually why I'm here." He opened the folder with the practiced motion of a man who has opened this folder in front of many business owners on many Tuesday afternoons. Membership forms, a newsletter, a calendar of events — the full Merchants Association welcome package, assembled with genuine care. "We'd like you in the fold, Lorri. You're good for Main Street. The foot traffic since you opened—"

"Has been good for everyone," I said.

"Has been good for everyone," he agreed. He looked at me with the directness of a man who has learned that getting to the point is more efficient than approaching it. "There's also something else."

"There usually is," I said.

He smiled — the civic smile, the one that meant he was about to ask for something and knew it. "We'd like to hold a Merchants Association meeting here. At Amorous. After hours — we'd be out of your way by ten. Private event, your house, your terms."

I looked at the room. I looked at the tables, generously spaced, the way they could be rearranged. I looked at Ginny's back, which was doing an excellent impression of a back that was not listening.

"How many members," I said.

"Eight. Maybe ten."

"On a Monday," I said. "We're quieter Mondays."

He nodded. "Monday works."

"And you'll want Ginny to run the bar."

"If she's willing."

Ginny set a bottle on the shelf without turning around. "I'm willing," she said.

Tom looked at her back with the expression of a man recalibrating his understanding of the room. "Good," he said.

"Susan Gregly will be there," he said, returning to me. "She's our treasurer. She's been wanting to come to Amorous since you opened."

"Everyone has been wanting to come to Amorous since we opened," I said. "Nobody comes until someone brings them."

"Consider this someone bringing her," he said.

* * *

I called Richard that evening.

"Tom Caulder came by," I said.

"I know," Richard said. "He called me first."

"Of course he did." I looked at my notes — the Monday date, the membership forms on the desk beside me. "The meeting makes sense. It's good civic positioning."

"It's good business," Richard said. "The Association has pull with P&Z. Caroline Fitch is a member in practice if not in name."

"Caroline will be there."

"Caroline will be there," Richard confirmed. "She's at everything."

I thought about a room full of Thornbury merchants after closing, the tables rearranged, Ginny behind the bar. I thought about Susan

Gregly, the antiques dealer two doors down, who had been a neighbor for eighteen months without becoming an acquaintance.

"Monday the fourteenth," I said.

"I'll be there," Richard said.

"Wear the jacket," I said.

A pause. "Which jacket."

"The good one," I said, and hung up.

* * *

The meeting was on a Monday evening in late July.

Lorri and Richard rearranged the tables themselves that afternoon — pushed the two-tops together in the center of the room, enough seating for twelve, the bar available for drinks before and after. Ginny set up with the efficiency of a woman who runs private events in her sleep. The dining room looked like what it was: a room that knew how to be more than one thing.

They came at seven. Tom first, then the others in ones and twos — merchants from Main Street and the surrounding blocks, the small-business fabric of a town that had worked very hard to remain the kind of town that had small-business fabric. A framing shop, a wine merchant, a woman who made custom stationery, a man who repaired clocks.

Caroline Fitch arrived at seven-ten, which was not fashionably late and not aggressively early — the timing of a First Selectman who understands that her arrival sets a temperature and calibrates accordingly. She was sixty-something, composed, the particular authority of a woman who has been in every room in Thornbury for twenty years and has never needed to announce herself in any of them. She looked at Amorous the way she looked at everything in Thornbury — completely, without comment.

"Lorri," she said, at the host stand.

"Caroline," I said.

"The building looks well," she said.

"The building is well," I said.

She smiled — brief, genuine — and went to find her seat.

Susan Gregly came last, at seven-fifteen, slightly breathless in the way of a woman who had closed her own shop twenty minutes ago and come directly. She was early-sixties, warm-faced, a cardigan over a blouse that suggested she had started the day with more optimism about the weather than the weather had deserved. She looked at the room and then at me with the frank appraisal of a woman who deals in old things and knows quality when she sees it.

"Susan Gregly," she said. "I'm two doors down and I've been meaning to introduce myself since April of last year."

"Lorri Oliver," I said. "I know. Tom mentioned you."

"Tom mentions everyone," she said. "It's his principal skill." She looked past me at the back-bar — the vinyl, the bottles, the VU meters glowing their quiet blue-green now that the evening had begun. "Oh," she said. "Oh, this is lovely."

"Come in," I said. "Ginny will get you something."

She came in. She found a seat. She looked at the room for the rest of the evening with the expression of a woman who appraises things for a living and has just found something worth appraising.

* * *

The meeting lasted two hours. It covered the matters that Merchants Association meetings cover — the Main Street repaving project, the holiday lighting schedule, a discussion about parking that had apparently been ongoing since 2019 and would continue indefinitely. Richard sat at the table and said the right things at the right moments with the calm authority of a man who has been in more meetings than most people and knows that the meeting is not the point.

The point was the room. The point was ten Thornbury merchants sitting in Amorous of Thornbury after hours with Ginny behind the bar and the vinyl playing and the candlelight doing its work, and all of them understanding, without being told, that this was a room worth protecting.

Phillip Richter from Voices arrived at eight-thirty with a camera and the professional enthusiasm of a man who recognizes a photograph when he sees one. He took three shots of the table — the merchants, the room, Richard and Lorri standing at the edge of the group with the back-bar behind them — and stayed for one drink and left at nine.

The photograph ran on the front page the following Thursday. Color. Above the fold.

Amorous of Thornbury hosts Merchants Association, the caption read. *Owner Lorri Oliver and co-owner Richard Wilkins welcome the Association to Main Street.*

Susan Gregly called on Friday morning to say she'd seen it.

"You looked good," she said.

"Richard chose the jacket," I said.

"He chose well," she said. "I'm coming to dinner next week. Is Tuesday available?"

"Tuesday is available," I said.

"Good," she said. "I have questions about the back-bar."

"Everyone has questions about the back-bar," I said.

"I have specific questions," she said, with the dry precision of a woman who means it. "I'll see you Tuesday."

Connecticut Magazine

Nora Briggs called on a Wednesday in August.

She was from the Litchfield County Tourism Board, she said, which in practice meant she was the Litchfield County Tourism Board — one person, a Subaru, and a camera bag, covering every inn and restaurant and covered bridge in the county with the focused enthusiasm of a woman who genuinely believes that what she's doing matters, which it does, which is what makes her simultaneously an asset and a problem.

"We're doing a fall feature," she said. "Litchfield County dining. Eight to ten restaurants. We'd love to include Amorous."

I thought about this for exactly as long as it deserved. "What does inclusion look like," I said.

"A visit," she said. "I'd come one evening, have dinner, take some photographs. A short writeup — three hundred words, maybe four. Connecticut Magazine runs it in the October issue."

"What photographs," I said.

A brief pause. "The room, primarily. The bar. The food. You and your co-owner if you're willing."

"The room," I said. "The bar. The food. Richard and I."

"If you're willing," she said again.

"Come on a Thursday," I said. "Early. Five-thirty, before we open. I'll show you what's worth showing."

* * *

She came on a Thursday in late August with her camera bag and her genuine enthusiasm and the particular energy of a woman who has photographed three hundred Connecticut restaurants and still finds each one interesting, which is either a professional gift or a form of optimism I hadn't encountered before.

I showed her the back-bar first. She photographed the vinyl cubbies, the bottles, the VU meters — three shots, different angles, the amber light doing the work it always does. She photographed the pendant lights and the tin ceiling and the original dark wood of the bar surface. She did not photograph the booths. I had not offered the booths and she had not asked, which meant either she hadn't noticed or she was more perceptive than most.

I suspected the latter.

Richard arrived at six. We stood together at the bar and Nora took two photographs — Richard in the good jacket, me in the hostess vest — with the back-bar behind us and the room in its pre-service quiet. Professional, warm, specific. The kind of photograph that says: *these people built something and know what they built.*

She stayed for dinner. She ate well and asked good questions and wrote in a small notebook with the focused attention of a woman who takes her three hundred words seriously. She left at eight-thirty with her camera bag and the promise that we'd see the piece before it ran. The wine had gone down well.

We saw it. It was three hundred and forty words. It was accurate. The photograph of Richard and me ran alongside it — the back-bar behind us, the room in its amber light, both of us looking like people who knew what they were doing.

The booths were not visible. The booth was not mentioned.

The piece ran in the October issue of Connecticut Magazine alongside seven other Litchfield County restaurants. Page forty-two. A good page.

* * *

I filed a copy in the office and didn't think much more about it.

Someone else did.

Sharon

Sharon Bruner had been in Thornbury for three weeks when she found Amorous.

She had found other things first — the hardware store, the wine merchant, the antiques dealer two buildings down from ATD who had regarded her Victorian with the careful neutrality of a professional deciding whether to be threatened. She had found the coffee shop and the library and the particular rhythm of a Main Street that took itself seriously without taking itself solemnly, which was harder to achieve than most towns understood.

She had not been looking for a restaurant.

She was looking at the facade.

Greek Revival, drawn blinds, no obvious entrance from Main Street. A building that faced the street without opening onto it — the architectural equivalent of a private conversation happening where anyone could see it was happening. She walked the facade, turned left into the parking lot, and found the door on the side.

Amorous, the sign read. Below it, in smaller type, the hours. The building was a converted Victorian — she knew Victorians now, knew them in the specific way of someone who had spent four months learning what a Victorian wanted to be when it grew up. This one had been listened to. The façade was exactly right: enough original detail to mean something, enough restraint to mean it quietly.

She went in.

* * *

The room stopped her.

Not the pink — she had been warned about the pink by nobody, because she knew nobody in Thornbury yet, which meant the pink arrived unannounced and landed as intended. It was the particular pink of a decision made by someone who understood that a color this committed required absolute confidence or it became a joke, and this was not a joke.

She stood in the vestibule and looked at the room.

The back-bar. The vinyl cubbies. The pendant lights. The dark wood. The tables spaced the way tables should be spaced — generously, as if the room understood that conversations needed room to breathe. Something playing from the cubbies that she placed after a moment: Bill Evans, *Waltz for Debby*, the Village Vanguard recording, a choice that was not accidental.

A woman in a gray hostess vest was moving through the dining room — stopping at a table, a hand on a shoulder, a brief exchange, laughter from the table that meant something had been said that landed exactly right. She moved to the next table. She was working the room the way someone works a room when the room is also theirs — not performing, not hosting in the service-industry sense. Something else. The ease of a woman in a space she built and knows completely.

Sharon watched her for a moment.

Then she sat at the bar.

* * *

The bartender was already there. Compact, still, the particular quality of a woman who had decided long ago that the bar was her territory and everything that happened in it happened because she allowed it. She looked at Sharon with the full assessment that takes one second when it's done correctly.

She poured something pale over ice and set it down.

She did not ask.

Sharon picked it up. Lillet Blanc, she thought, and confirmed it on the second sip. The bartender had looked at her for one second and poured Lillet.

She set the glass down and watched the woman in the vest cross the room again — a different table now, the same ease, the same quality of attention that made each table feel like the only one.

"How long has she been doing this?" Sharon said.

The bartender picked up a glass.

"Doing what?" she said.

One beat.

Sharon smiled.

"Right," she said.

The bartender set the glass down. She picked up another one and began to polish it with the unhurried attention of a woman who had just completed a transaction she found satisfactory.

* * *

I came out of the office at seven forty-five because Ginny had appeared in the doorway.

She does this sometimes — appears without knocking, stands in the frame for a moment, and either speaks or doesn't. When she doesn't speak it means the dining room is fine and she's simply reporting in. When she does speak it means something requires my attention, stated in the minimum number of words that will convey it.

She stood in the doorframe.

"Bar," she said.

I set down the October schedule.

* * *

She was on the corner stool — the one that gives you the full room without committing to the room, the one I think of privately as the assessment seat because it's where people sit when they're not sure yet whether they're staying. She was in her forties, platinum blonde, the particular groomed quality of a woman who understands presentation as a discipline rather than a vanity. Pearl-and-gold at her wrist. Diamond tennis bracelet. A fitted black sweater that had cost what it cost and didn't announce it. She was holding a glass of Lillet over ice — Ginny's pour, which meant Ginny had looked at her and decided, which meant something had already happened at this bar that I hadn't witnessed.

She was looking at the back-bar.

Not the way people usually look at the back-bar — the civilian's appreciation, the tourist's wonder. She was reading it. The vinyl cubbies, the bottles, the VU meters in their quiet blue-green. The way someone reads a room they're trying to understand from the inside out.

I came to the bar and she heard me before I reached her — she had that quality, the awareness of a woman who has been in enough rooms to know where the room is moving — and she turned.

Brown eyes. Blue contacts over brown eyes, which I registered and noted and did not comment on, because we all construct our faces and the construction is nobody's business but the constructor's.

She looked at me the way I had just looked at her — a complete assessment, one pass, nothing missed. Then she smiled. It was the smile of a woman who had found something she was looking for without knowing she was looking for it.

"You built this," she said.

It was not a question.

"Richard helped," I said.

"Richard," she said, with the tone of a woman filing a name.

"Co-owner." I sat down on the stool beside her. "Lorri Oliver."

"Sharon Bruner." She picked up her glass. "I'm two buildings down. I bought the Victorian in September."

I looked at her. "Antiques to Desire," I said.

Something shifted in her expression — not surprise, recalibration. A piece of information landing in a file she'd started. "You know it," she said.

"I know the sign," I said. "I haven't been in."

"Nobody's been in," she said. "That's the point." She looked at her glass. "Appointment only."

"The sign says that."

"Most people don't read signs," she said.

"Most people," I agreed.

She looked at the back-bar and then at me with the directness of a woman who had been in enough rooms to have stopped being indirect some time ago. "What's in the vinyl," she said.

"Jazz, primarily. Some soul. A little country when Ginny's feeling pluralistic."

"She chose the Bill Evans record."

"Ginny chooses everything," I said. "I make suggestions. She considers them."

Sharon looked at Ginny, who was at the far end of the bar doing what Ginny does at the far end of the bar — present, attending, appearing not to listen, which is the most efficient form of listening. "How long has she been with you," Sharon said.

"Since we opened. April 2023."

"She poured my drink without asking."

"She does that."

"She got it right."

"She always gets it right," I said. "I've stopped trying to understand how."

Sharon picked up her glass. "I had a woman in New Haven," she said. "Different work. Same quality. You spend twenty years trying to figure out how they do what they do and eventually you accept that some things operate outside your understanding and your job is to keep them happy so they stay."

I looked at her. "Twenty years in New Haven," I said.

"Approximately." She took a small sip. "I came here for something different."

"Did you find it?"

She looked at the room — the candlelight, the tables, the particular atmosphere of a Tuesday at Amorous when everything was working the way it was built to work. She looked at the back-bar. She looked at me.

"I'm working on it," she said.

The Bill Evans track ended. Ginny put on something else without consulting anyone — *Corcovado*, Getz and Gilberto, the warm bossa drifting in over the saxophone — and the room resettled around it.

"You came in alone," I said.

"I go most places alone," she said. "It's easier to see."

"See what."

She smiled — not the smile from before, something smaller and more private. "What's worth coming back to," she said.

I picked up the glass Ginny had set in front of me at some point in the last five minutes without my noticing — Sancerre, my glass, appearing the way things appear when Ginny decides they should. I looked at Sharon Bruner on the corner stool with her Lillet and her blue contacts and her diamond tennis bracelet and the expression of a woman who had built something from nothing and was quietly assessing whether what I had built was worth the time it would take to understand it.

"Come back on a Thursday," I said. "We're livelier Thursdays."

"What's the difference," she said.

"Thursday," I said, "Ginny occasionally smiles."

Sharon looked at Ginny. Ginny was polishing a glass with the focused attention of a woman who was not listening and had heard every word.

Sharon laughed — the real kind, the kind that arrives before you can decide whether to let it, the kind that means something caught you off guard and you didn't mind. It was a good laugh. The laugh of a woman who had not laughed this way in longer than she would have said.

I thought: *I like her.*

Then I thought: that's not quite it.

I filed it and picked up my Sancerre.

* * *

She left at nine. She put on her jacket with the motion of a woman who has decided, shook my hand once — a real handshake, brief, the kind that means something — and walked through the dining room and through the vestibule without looking back.

Ginny watched her go.

She picked up Sharon's glass. She held it for a moment — not quite looking at it, not quite not looking at it — and set it in the rack below the bar.

She picked up a fresh glass and began to polish it.

"Thursday," she said.

"Yes," I said.

She polished the glass. The VU meters held their quiet blue-green. The Getz and Gilberto played on from the cubbies, unhurried, doing what Ginny had intended it to do.

I sat at the bar for a while after the room cleared and thought about a woman who had arrived in Thornbury alone and walked Main Street until she found the right door and gone in. Who had sat at the corner stool and read the back-bar like a text and laughed at the right moment without calculating whether to.

I thought about the Victorian two buildings down with its *appointment only* sign and its owner who went most places alone because it was easier to see.

There was something there I didn't have language for yet.

That was fine. Some things you understand later.

Vincent

He called on a Friday in October.

I was in the office. The Connecticut Magazine issue had been out for two weeks and I had stopped thinking about it, which is when things that come from it tend to happen.

"Lorri Oliver," I said.

"Ms. Oliver." A pause — not Wayne's pause, not the craftsman's ease with silence. This was a different kind of pause. The pause of a man choosing his first words with professional care. "My name is Vincent Renzi. I have a restaurant in Ridgefield. Renzi's, on Route 7. I don't know if you'd know it."

I knew it. Thirty-three years of selling kitchens in Fairfield County — I knew every restaurant worth knowing between Greenwich and Danbury. Renzi's had been on Route 7 since the early nineties. Intimate room, northern Italian, the kind of place that doesn't need to advertise because the people who know about it tell the people who should know about it.

"I know it," I said.

A brief silence that meant he was pleased. "I saw the Connecticut Magazine piece," he said. "The photograph. I recognized you from the RBA years — you came through Ridgefield several times. I don't know if you remember."

I remembered Ridgefield. I did not specifically remember Vincent Renzi, which I did not say. "The RBA years cover a lot of territory," I said.

"They do," he said. "I've been meaning to come to Amorous since I saw the piece. I'd like to see what you've built." A pause. "And I'd like to call ahead rather than simply appear."

I looked at the office wall — the copy of the Connecticut Magazine piece pinned there, Richard and me at the bar, the back-bar behind us. Page forty-two. A good page.

"Come on a Tuesday," I said. "We're quieter Tuesdays."

"What time," he said.

"Whenever you like," I said. "It's an hour from Ridgefield. Come when the drive suits you."

"I'll come in October," he said.

"October is a good month for the drive," I said.

"It is," he said. And then: "Thank you, Ms. Oliver."

"Lorri," I said.

Another pause — shorter. "Lorri," he said.

* * *

He came on a Tuesday evening in late October.

I didn't know he was there.

This is the thing about Amorous on a Tuesday — it runs itself, or close enough. Martin in the kitchen, Ginny behind the bar, the dining room at two-thirds capacity with the regulars who have made Tuesday their night because Tuesday at Amorous is quieter and they know what quiet in this room means. I was in the office going over the November schedule when Ginny knocked once on the doorframe and leaned in.

She looked at me for one second.

"There's a man at the bar," she said.

I looked up. Ginny does not announce men at the bar. Men at the bar are her territory and she manages them without commentary. The fact that she was in my doorway meant something.

"What kind of man," I said.

She considered this with the seriousness it deserved. "The kind," she said, "that didn't ask for you."

I set down the November schedule.

* * *

He was at the far end of the bar — the corner stool, the one that gives you the full room without putting your back to the door. Dark jacket, open collar, no tie. Dark hair silver at the temples, still thick. Olive complexion, clean-shaven. He was looking at the back-bar with the attention of a man who knows what he's looking at — not a civilian's appreciation, not a tourist's wonder. A professional's assessment. He was reading the room the way I would read a room.

He had a glass of something amber in front of him that Ginny had chosen, which meant she had looked at him and decided.

He hadn't asked for me. He was simply there, present and unhurried, letting the room be what it was.

I came out of the office and walked to the bar and he saw me before I reached him — the moment of recognition arriving in stages, the way it does when you're placing someone from a different context in a different decade. He didn't stand. He simply went still, the way a man goes still when the thing he came for has arrived and he doesn't want to disturb it by moving too quickly.

I sat down on the stool beside him.

We looked at the back-bar together for a moment — the vinyl cubbies, the bottles, the VU meters glowing their blue-green in the amber shadow. Ginny at the far end, polishing a glass, not looking at us, which meant she was watching everything.

"Vincent Renzi," he said.

"Lorri Oliver," I said.

"I know," he said.

We sat with that. The music played from the cubbies — something unhurried that Ginny had selected with full intention and would describe, if asked, as having come up on shuffle. The dining room moved around us at its own pace.

He had a chef's hands — I noticed them on the glass. Scarred, capable, the hands of a man who has been in professional kitchens for forty years and carries the evidence of it in every knuckle. He held the glass with the particular ease of a man comfortable with good things.

"The back-bar," he said.

"Yes," I said.

"The vinyl is real."

"It's real," I said. "Two sources. The house we bought it from and my own collection. Thirty years of collecting during the radio years."

He looked at me. "Radio."

"WNCZ," I said. "New Canaan. Jazz Scape. Before the RBA."

Something shifted in his expression — not surprise, recognition. A piece of information landing in a file he'd already started. "I listened to that station," he said.

"A lot of people listened to that station," I said.

"Not everyone who hosted it ended up running a restaurant in Thornbury," he said.

"No," I said. "Just me."

He smiled — the slow kind, the kind that starts somewhere private and arrives on the face a moment later. He looked at the room — the candlelight, the tables, the particular atmosphere of a Tuesday at Amorous when the room is doing what it was built to do.

"You built this well," he said.

"Thirty-three years of other people's kitchens," I said. "It turns out to be useful."

"It turns out to be useful," he agreed, and looked at his glass, and looked at the back-bar, and looked at me with the directness of a man who has driven an hour on a Tuesday evening in October and has decided he did not drive an hour to be indirect.

"I've only seen you in business suits," he said.

I looked at the hostess vest. The starched white blouse. The bowtie at my collar. "Business suits are for business," I said.

He smiled.

"This," I said, "is for something else."

He held my gaze across the bar in the amber light and the music from the cubbies and the particular Tuesday quiet of a room that had been built for exactly this kind of moment, among others.

"Pleasure," I said.

He smiled. "Pleasure," he said.

* * *

We sat at the bar for twenty minutes. We talked about Ridgefield and Thornbury and the particular challenge of running an intimate restaurant in a small Connecticut town in an era that did not always reward intimacy or smallness. We talked about the RBA years — the kitchens we had both walked, the chefs we had both known, the particular language of people who have spent decades in the trade and recognize each other by it.

He did not touch his glass again after the first twenty minutes. He was not there for the drink.

At the end of the twenty minutes he set the glass down with the finality of a man who has decided.

"I'd like to have dinner here," he said. "With you, if you'll have me."

I looked at him across the bar — the scarred capable hands, the silver at the temples, the directness of a man who drove an hour on a Tuesday to say exactly this and nothing more.

I heard both sentences. I answered the one that mattered.

"Call me," I said. "We'll find an evening."

He nodded once. He put on his jacket. He thanked Ginny, who accepted this with a brief inclination of her head that constituted her highest form of acknowledgment.

At the door he turned. He looked at the room one more time — the back-bar in its amber shadow, the candles, the Tuesday quiet of it — and then he looked at me at the bar.

He nodded once more. Then he was gone.

* * *

Ginny set down her glass.

She picked up another one.

She polished it for a long moment without speaking, which from Ginny is its own kind of speech.

"Ridgefield," she said finally.

"Yes," I said.

She polished the glass. The VU meters held their quiet blue-green. Somewhere in the dining room a couple was finishing dessert, unhurried, unaware that anything had just happened at the bar.

"An hour away," Ginny said.

"About that," I said.

She set the glass down. She looked at me with the expression she reserves for moments when one word is not quite enough but two is still sufficient.

"Good," she said.

She went back to work. I sat at the bar for a while longer and looked at the back-bar in its amber light and thought about a phone call in October and a man who had not asked for me and had not needed to.

The fork was on the table.

I had not picked it up. I had not put it down. I had simply noted that it was there, which for now was enough.

The Car He Kept

The man selling it wanted two hundred dollars. Wayne had eighty-seven.

He'd found it on a Tuesday in March of 1980, parked on a side street in Stamford with a handwritten card in the windshield. *1960 Chev. Runs. Call Ray.* He'd called Ray from a pay phone on the corner and stood there in the cold with his hand wrapped around the receiver and looked at the car while it rang.

Ray wanted two hundred. Wayne had eighty-seven. He told Ray this. Ray said come look at it anyway, which Wayne understood to mean that Ray also wanted to be done with it.

He looked at it for twenty minutes. The exterior was sound — the fire engine red still vivid under the March light, the chrome intact, the convertible top faded but holding. The interior was another matter. The seat material was split along the driver's side, the door panels soft with age, the dashboard cracked in two places. A lesser eye would have seen damage. Wayne ran his hand along the door panel and felt what was underneath — the bones of it, the structure, the specific quality of a thing built to last that had simply been sat in for twenty years by people who didn't know what they had.

He knew what it was. He couldn't have said how he knew. His hands knew before he did.

He offered Ray one hundred and ten dollars — everything he had plus what he could borrow from his brother by Thursday. Ray looked at the car and then at the boy standing next to it and said yes, which was the right answer. The yes had something to do with the price and something to do with the way the boy had spent twenty minutes with his hand on the door panel before saying a word.

The previous owner had pulled the original column shift and installed a four-speed floor shift, which was a common thing to do in the sixties and a reasonable thing to do if you knew what you were doing, which this particular man had not entirely known. First gear was gone.

This was why Ray was selling. Wayne knew this when he handed over the money.

He drove it home in second gear. The bench seat held him. The engine ran its steady note. He pulled into his parents' driveway and sat in the car for a moment after he cut the engine, the way you sit with something you've just understood.

He didn't know what he'd do with it yet. He didn't know about the upholstery — the trade that would come from watching what needed to be done and learning to do it. He didn't know about the drive-ins or the car shows or the forty-four years of a Connecticut life with this car in it.

He was seventeen. He had a car.

He knew it was worth keeping.

That was enough.

The Kitchen He Built

The grandfather arrived at Ellis Island in 1911 with one bag and the contents of his mother's kitchen carried entirely in memory. He was twenty-two. He understood, standing on that dock in the January cold, that the memory was already imperfect and would only become more so. He decided to carry it anyway. Faithfully. As far as it would go.

He went to Norwalk. The mills were hiring. He rented two rooms in a building full of men who had made the same crossing and brought the same determination, and he cooked what he remembered of his mother's kitchen on a two-burner stove and fed it to whoever was at the table.

His son — Vincent's father — was born in Norwalk in 1927, grew up between two languages, came home from the war a sergeant, used the GI Bill to buy a Cape Cod three streets from where he'd grown up, and went to work in manufacturing with the organizational precision the Army had given him and the ambition the grandfather had carried across the ocean. He worked his way up. He did well. He paid for two daughters' weddings — the expensive Italian kind, the kind the grandfather would have recognized — and watched his only son go to work in other people's kitchens.

Vincent spent his twenties cooking for men who owned rooms he didn't own yet. Norwalk. Bridgeport. Stamford. The work of learning a trade from the inside — the heat, the hours, the specific education of a professional kitchen that no business degree could provide. He learned what he didn't know. By his early thirties he knew what he needed to know.

The father did not hesitate. He had spent thirty years earning the right to write one check that mattered.

They found the room together — a failing restaurant on a good Ridgefield street, older, tired, the owners ready to be done with it. Good bones. The father saw a building. Vincent saw the grandfather's kitchen, finally, with four walls around it. They had friends in construction who understood the difference between a price and a family price. The room was renovated correctly and opened as Renzi's in 1992.

Vincent cooked in it for more than thirty years.

He cooked the grandmother's kitchen — imperfectly, faithfully, two generations and an ocean removed from the source, translated twice before it reached his hands, and he translated it again each night into plates that went out to Connecticut strangers who did not know what they were eating was an act of recovery. He did not tell them. The food told them, or it didn't, and either way he had done what the grandfather decided on that dock in January 1911.

He carried it as far as it would go.

Last year he handed the keys to his sons.

He had expected relief. He had expected grief. He had not expected both at the same time, arriving together without warning, and he had not expected the specific feeling of a man whose hands have carried something for thirty years discovering, on an ordinary Tuesday in October, that his hands are empty.

He drove an hour north to a restaurant in Thornbury he'd read about in a magazine.

He sat at the bar.

He did not ask for anyone.

Visit SomethingInTheWaterSeries.com
Learn more about Thornbury and what's coming next.

Scan to visit SomethingInTheWaterSeries.com

Also Available

The Yearbook & The Impala — Books One and Two

Lorri Oliver opened a restaurant at sixty and her second adolescence at the same time. The combined first volume of the Something In The Water series.

About the Author

The Something In The Water series grew from a simple observation: that women of a certain age have stories that are funny and warm and occasionally breathtaking, and that nobody had been telling them quite right.

She lives in the Litchfield Hills of Connecticut.

Also by Lorri Ryan Oliver

Something In The Water
The Yearbook
The Impala
Wayne

Watch for more at https://somethinginthewaterseries.com/.

About the Author

Lorri Ryan Oliver has spent most of her adult life feeding people — first as a restaurant industry professional, and later as the owner of a small restaurant in a small Connecticut town that somehow became the center of a very large world.

She came to writing the way most people come to the things that matter — sideways, late, and wondering why it took so long.

The *Something In The Water* series grew from a simple observation: that women of a certain age have stories that are funny and warm and occasionally breathtaking, and that nobody had been telling them quite right.

She is doing her best to fix that.

Lorri lives in the Litchfield Hills area of Connecticut, where the autumn lasts exactly as long as it should and the coffee is always on and the stories never run out.

Read more at https://somethinginthewaterseries.com/.

www.ingramcontent.com/pod-product-compliance
Lightning Source LLC
LaVergne TN
LVHW090617110826
845146LV00001B/426

* 9 7 9 8 9 9 5 3 4 3 1 4 1 *